From Here to There

by Mona Shea Frasier
illustrated by Anne Kennedy

Harcourt

Orlando   Boston   Dallas   Chicago   San Diego

Visit *The Learning Site!*

www.harcourtschool.com

Jill and her dad were in a field near their house. They were sitting on a grassy hill, looking up at the stars. The stars were so bright. They looked like a sprinkling of diamonds.

Jill sighed. She looked at her dad and said, "I feel so small."

"Small!" said her dad. "There are a lot of things that are smaller than you and me. Do you know how small an atom is? Now that's small."

"How small is an atom?" Jill asked.

"Well, look at the tip of your finger. Billions of atoms make up that fingertip!" her dad explained.

"That's small all right!" Jill agreed, studying her fingertip. "I'm big compared to an atom. But when I look up at the stars, I wonder about my place in the universe. It's so big out there."

"Small things are part of bigger things," said her dad. "You live in a house. You have a room in the house. So one part of your place is your room in our house. Are you with me so far?"

"Yes," said Jill. She was not sure where this was going.

"Next," said her dad, "your house is on Franklin Street. Franklin Street is in a neighborhood. The entire neighborhood is called Oak Hill. So you are from our house, which is number 345, and our street, which is Franklin Street, and our neighborhood, which is Oak Hill. But that's not all, Jill," said her dad.

"You know the birds that come to our feeder. You know the trees you climb on in the Jacksons' yard. You know where your school, the library, the supermarket, and the fire station are. So, your place is this neighborhood."

"I knew that, Dad," Jill said.

"But your place is more than just the neighborhood," said her dad. "Your neighborhood is part of Summit County. People know this county because of the mountains here. So if you say you are from Summit County, people will say, 'Ah. She comes from the mountains.'"

"So that's my place? The mountains?"

"Yes," said Jill's father, "but there's more."

"You live in the state of Colorado. So you are from Summit County in the state of Colorado. Colorado is in a country called the United States. The United States is on the continent of North America, one of the seven continents."

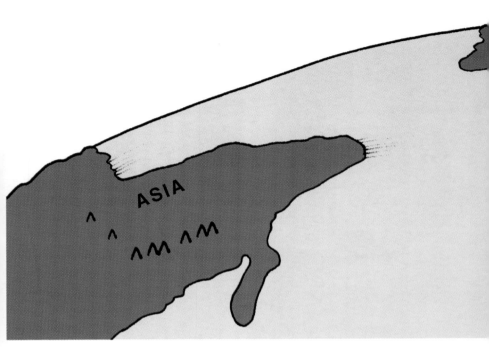

"It's in a song," Jill said. "'North America, South America, Africa, Europe, Asia. Don't forget Antarctica, don't forget Australia.'"

"So you are from Colorado in the United States on the continent of North America," her dad said.

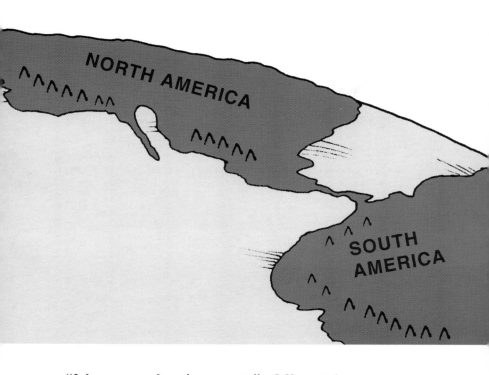

"I know what's next," Jill said.
"Eventually, this gets even bigger. I can say
I'm from the planet Earth. Earth is a really
big place."

"Yet it's a small sphere, spinning in
space," said her dad.

"Big or small, it's our sphere," Jill said.

"Yes," her father said. "You are a
resident of the planet Earth."

Jill asked, "Is there more?"

"Yes," her father answered. "That's still not the entire picture. Let's say you eventually go into space, as you've always dreamed of doing. Your spacecraft will lift off and travel through the atmosphere. After you leave the atmosphere, you'll be in space."

"What will I see?" Jill asked.

"You'll see the moon. You'll see other objects in space."

"What is in space?" Jill wanted to know.

"Stars. Comets. Asteroids. Planets. The sun. They all travel through space," Jill's dad said.

"But how do I belong to them?" Jill asked.

"They are part of the solar system that Earth belongs to. In it, nine planets and other objects travel around a star that we call the sun."

"Doesn't everyone call it the sun?" Jill asked.

"Not if you're in another solar system," her dad said. "Our sun and planets are in a galaxy called the Milky Way. There are 500,000 million stars in the Milky Way."

"Is there more beyond that?" Jill asked.

"The Milky Way is one of about 100,000 million galaxies," Jill's dad said. "Earth is a part of the entire universe."

"Wow!" Jill exclaimed. She was quiet for a moment. "If we were heading homeward from one of those galaxies, it would take a while, wouldn't it?"

"Oh, yes," her father said. "But right now, let's head homeward ourselves."

"I know my place in the universe now," Jill said. "It's big out there, isn't it?"

"Yes," said her dad, "but remember, you have a special place in this big universe!"